LIMER

D0487443

3 00

Elias Martin
Published in Great Britain in 2017
by Graffeg Limited

Written by Nicola Davies
copyright © 2017.
Illustrated by Fran Shum
copyright © 2017.
Designed and produced by Graffeg
Limited copyright © 2017

Graffeg Limited, 24 Stradey Park
Business Centre, Mwrwg Road,
Llangennech, Llanelli, Carmarthenshire
SA14 8YP Wales UK
Tel 01554 824000 www.graffeg.com

Nicola Davies is hereby identified as the
author of this work in accordance with
section 77 of the Copyrights, Designs and
Patents Act 1988.

A CIP Catalogue record for this book is
available from the British Library.

All rights reserved. No part of this
publication may be reproduced, stored
in a retrieval system or transmitted, in
any form or by any means, electronic,
mechanical, photocopying, recording or
otherwise, without the prior permission
of the publishers.

ISBN 9781910862506

1 2 3 4 5 6 7 8 9

NICOLA DAVIES
ELIAS MARTIN

ILLUSTRATION FRAN SHUM

for Maggie Benfield and Bryan Doubt

WITHDRAWN FROM STOCK

GRAFFEG

TIMBERLINE CITY LIBRARY

ELIAS MARTIN

Follow the Pole Star far enough and you'll come to a land where every winter is a test. Snow lies thick on the ground from October to April. Frost will bite at your fingers and gnaw at your face. Winter in this place allows no second chances and there are several varieties of death always easily to hand.

And yet there is life here. Life made ingenious by eons of trial. Life made determined. Life that will not quit.

Some have always been drawn to the North by the challenge of survival in such a tough place. A century or so ago they came as gold prospectors, lumberjacks and fur trappers, seeking a place where a man could shape his own destiny, and not have it handed to him from the shelves of a shop. Elias Martin was among them, but he came North for a different reason: abandoned by his parents and hounded on the wrong side of the law, he was driven North by dint of not fitting in anywhere else. By the time he washed up to the door of a one-roomed log cabin, in the remote backwoods of a northern province, he knew this was his last chance in life. He carried a fur trapper's licence, a bag of steel traps, a rifle and the conviction that all of nature was his personal enemy. He was seventeen years old.

Elias knew something about surviving in the remote backwoods, but it was not nearly enough. The first winter he almost froze to death because he had put his wood store too far from the cabin door. When it fell to 30 below, he risked frostbite every time he needed to feed his stove. The second winter, he almost starved because his deer meat wasn't properly dried; it rotted to a putrid mess. The third winter, he did alright, but when he went to the trading post with his furs, he was robbed on the trail and lost everything.

But Elias had learned the first lesson of the North: that quitting was not a possibility.

He bought new traps and a rifle on credit and went back to his trade of murdering creatures even hungrier than himself. He took their crushed bodies from between the steel teeth and skinned the corpses with a kind of relish. With every one he felt a tiny victory against the wild that had tried to kill him and the world that had turned its back on him.

In ten years, he grew a scowl that never left his face and a reputation for determination as biting and steely as the teeth of a trap. He lived for trapping, for his own endless war against life, driven by the lonely darkness in his soul. At first, other trappers spat on the ground at the mention of his name, 'Elias Martin, that miserable cuss!' But at last, they shrugged and shook their heads, moved by something between pity and dread.

One night, in his twelfth year in the North, there came an early fall of snow. Elias went out into the darkness to inspect it, glad that tracking his prey would soon grow easier.

There were tracks on the clear ground between his cabin and the wood store, although his sharp senses had detected nothing, and his old hound lay asleep on the porch. He fetched a lantern to examine the marks more closely. They didn't lead out of the woods, or up from the river, they appeared from nowhere, like those of a bird, landing on the ground. But they were not the tracks of a bird, or of any animal, but those of small, bare, human feet.

With a racing heart, Elias followed them to his woodshed and found a child, very small and ragged, curled up asleep on a pile of logs. He stared at the child for a long, long time. All manner of tides and currents he'd thought long dried were running anew in his heart. Then, gently, he picked her up.

There was no blizzard then or the next day. The snow lay light and even, undrifted. It would have been the easiest task to take the child to the trading post and leave her where she could be

most easily reclaimed by whoever had lost her. Yet Elias found every excuse not to do so: a blizzard could hit and strand him, keeping him from his traps; the child's people could come looking for her close to where she had been lost. Besides, the child herself gave no sign of feeling lost, or being in any way distressed. She showed, instead, every sign of being perfectly at home.

Elias made a little curtained room for her, in the warm corner, nearest the fire. He built a box bed and covered it with a sable fur blanket. When she slept, he watched over her and sometimes touched her dark, smooth hair with one finger. He would have smiled, if anyone had ever taught him how.

Elias named her Birch, because something in him noticed that her eyes were the colour of that tree's new born leaves, and that that was a good thing. He had not the first idea how to raise a child, having never been raised himself. But he tried. He fed her, clothed her as best he could, and spoke as kindly to her as he could manage. Little by little, she began to speak back. Elias took her out into the woods with him and tried to give her all the skills and knowledge that his hard life had made him learn.

Birch was quick and clever, and although she was too small to do heavy work, her nimble fingers and sharp eyes were useful in a hundred ways. She could move silently through the landscape and had a feeling for its creatures and their ways. By spring she was an indispensable helper. Elias and Birch spent the summer hunting, picking berries, plants and mushrooms and drying them, laying up stores of food to keep them fed through the long, cold months. Then came the winter, the time for trapping, and still Birch helped, though it was Elias who did all the skinning and curing.

Seasons came and went and with two pairs of hands, there seemed to Elias to be more time to

notice things. He did not remember ever having felt the warmth of his stove, or breathed the promising smell of roasting deer meat. He did not remember having heard the first trickle of the thawing stream in spring, or seen how the midsummer sunset slanted between the trees. But with Birch, he noticed all of these things.

Birch herself noted every detail of the world around her and pointed them out to Elias. And she smiled. Under that kind of sunshine, even the coldest ice must melt. Sometimes, Elias even smiled back, although his smile didn't show so well on his face.

A few times in the year, they made the day-long journey to the trading post to barter skins for stores and ammunition, and make a little money over. No one ever asked where Birch had come from, accepting her as just another part of Elias Martin's strangeness, but the trade post manager, who all the trappers called Captain, treated Birch like a princess.

He sat her on the counter and fed her spoons of maple syrup.

Birch never asked for anything and it never crossed Elias' mind that she would want anything. So, once, when Captain made her a gift of a penknife, well made, but fitted to the child's small hands, her pleasure stung Elias like a wasp. He scowled at Captain when they left and didn't bid him goodbye. All the way home he stilled Birch's chatter with his silence, and didn't comment when she spent the evening holed up in her box bed. But, when he found a tiny fox, perfectly carved from firewood, on his pillow, his heart hurt so much he had to press his hand hard into his chest to make it stop. He poured extra syrup on Birch's grits the next morning.

That winter was a good one for trapping. Almost every day brought new additions to the stack of pelts in the fur store.

Birch stood back when Elias set the traps and then, later, collected the bodies, but she never protested her disapproval. Yet, more and more, Elias felt it.

Once, he found her crying over the cured skins in the fur store and scolded her for foolishness. She dried her tears and no more was said about it, but from that day her menagerie of wooden animals grew: foxes, martens, bears, bobcats, beavers. For every animal whose bloodied, broken body Elias wrenched from the sharp jaws of his traps, Birch made a carving. She carved the details, not only of every kind of animal but of every individual: the fox whose ear had been notched, the bear with the scar over its eye. Every one was recreated, to dance along the roof beams of the cabin, or perch above the stove. They were so alive, Elias began to feel they were watching him.

Then, one morning, close to the turn of the year, they went to check the trapline together, and found each trap wrenched open, emptied. Elias could see from Birch's face that she believed the animals had escaped. But he knew better.

The space around each trap was covered in tracks, flat footed and long clawed. 'Wolverine,' Elias told Birch, 'Wolverine.' The word was like a poison on his tongue. A wolverine was no larger than a hound, and low slung like a weasel, but it was a demon with power and cunning far beyond its stature. It would wreck his traps again and again, even raid his food and fur store. He must kill the wolverine now, right away, or be destroyed.

Grim-faced, he marched back to the cabin with Birch struggling to keep up. He stocked the cabin with firewood and food, told Birch to stay inside until he returned, and then he left. Inside him, his bitter battle with the world flowed again, like molten ice. It froze away Birch's tears and fearful pleadings for him to stay. It froze away all but the desire for the moment when the wolverine would lie dead at his feet.

LIMERICK CITY AND COUNTY LIBRARY

00501202

The wolverine was a big male, strong, and confident in its ability to survive. Its trail lead directly up the mountain. Doggedly, Elias followed up and out, onto the barren, high ground above, followed for two days without a halt before a blizzard struck. Blinding white at first, then utter blackness as the night came down. He crouched among rocks for protection, whilst the wind screeched around him. He ground his teeth, for the snow would cover up and scour away the trail. This time, the wolverine had escaped him! As the frightful, howling snowstorm filled up the world, a thought melted through the ice of his resolve: Birch! Birch, all alone in the terror of this blizzard. His insides turned to water. Of all the many foolish, wicked, purely stupid things with which he felt he'd filled his life, leaving Birch alone in the cabin was suddenly, clearly, worst of all.

It took four days to make it home. Two through the blizzard, and two of cruel struggle through three feet of new fallen, powder snow and his growing fear for Birch. He reached the cabin at dusk. The yard was crossed with the fresh prints, not two hours old, of a wolverine, the same big male that he'd been tracking, he was sure. Their old hound lay dead in the yard, its throat ripped out, and the foodstore door was open – what the wolverine couldn't eat, it had spoiled with its foul scent. Birch was gone. The cabin was stone cold and empty. The imprint of her small snowboots, criss-crossed with the wolverine's tracks, laced the snow, but lead nowhere.

Frantic, calling her name until his voice cracked, Elias went back and forth trying to make sense of the trail she'd left, trying to work out which way she might have gone. But her footprints lead nowhere, they simply ended in the encircling blank of snow. Just as her arrival in his life had made no sense, it seemed neither did her departure.

He lay on the cold hearth and took a few hours rest. At first light he set off, following the only clear trail, that of the wolverine, the demon creature, who, Elias felt, had taken Birch away.

The wolverine, like all wolverines, was the very soul of the North. An animal with no quit in it. Well fed now, it moved fast, even in the deep snow where Elias cursed and struggled. Elias knew he would fall more and more behind, but he would catch up with the creature. He would.

It travelled in a straight line for five days and took Elias into country he had never seen before. High forests of stunted, spindly trees, and treacherous ravines, hidden with snow. In this new place it slowed down and began to hunt. Elias found fresh kills, and bones, long dead, dug up and crunched to dust. The wolverine would eat anything. Elias kept his distance, learning the wolverine's ways. Every part of him, every ounce of energy was focused on the demon, keeping

his thoughts away at all costs from Birch, Birch, Birch, and where she might have gone. Inside, his soul chanted for the wolverine's death. He slept only in snatches and dreamed of footprints, the line of bare feet appearing from nowhere, the line of tiny boot-prints disappearing into unmarked snow.

The wolverine would rip any steel trap apart, and Elias knew he would never get close enough for a good shot. So he built a deadfall trap; a thunder of logs to crush the creature to death. He baited it with beaver and made a lure of fish oil and rotting deerskin, to spread a tempting smell to draw the wolverine in. Then he moved back, two hours' march, and waited, leaning in the thin, winter sunlight against a tree, trying to stay awake and failing.

Birch came to him. Barefoot across the snow. Her green eyes danced like leaves. 'Why do you fight the wild?' she asked, and walked away when he had no answer.

Elias woke. Somehow, he knew the trap was sprung. The moon had not yet risen but the stars were bright enough to cast blue tree-shadows, fingerlike, across the milky snow.

Over a frozen lake, up a snow filled canyon, he trudged. Owls called in the trees; far off, a pack of wolves staked out their territory with a chorus of howling. Elias' eyes were tuned to darkness now and, near to the trap, he picked up the wolverine's trail. Big feet, long claws, with the dust-like imprint of thick, winter fur around each one.

The trap was up a small rise, in a clearing, where lightning had felled a knot of trees. Elias could see its outline and could tell it had, indeed, been sprung. His heart leaped. He slowed his pace to savour the story that the tracks told, of the wolverine's last steps in this world, anticipating the moment when the creature would, at last, lie dead before him. The tracks dipped into shadow and then emerged in glowing starlight, deep blue-black against the snow.

Elias' heart stood still. Beside the wolverine's trail, there was a line of other footprints, tiny snow boots, whose wearer leant a little bit towards her wolverine companion, almost as if she rested one hand on its back. There could be no mistake. The two sets of tracks, child and wolverine, lead right to the deadfall and inside. There had been no escape. No reprieve.

Elias ran the last few feet, crying out. It had taken two days of back breaking effort to lift the heavy logs into place, but now, with fearful strength, Elias threw the fallen logs aside like sticks. Gasping with tears, wretching with the horror of what he was about to find, the broken body, the bloodied little boots, he stood for a moment utterly bewildered at what truly lay there.

Behind him, the moon rose at last and shone bright onto the scattered mess of logs, onto the sad patch of muddied snow that the trap had crushed.

No bodies. Not a speck of blood, or fur or bone. No little boots. Instead, two small, wooden figures, side by side. A wolverine, not demon like, but wild and noble, and a child, barefoot and ragged, with wide bright eyes.

Elias cradled them in his hands and looked out over the clearing at the snowy land that lay beyond the wreckage of his trap. The beauty of the moonlit landscape hurt him so hard he had to press the little wooden figures to his heart to make it stop. He looked out over the silver and blue, and saw a line of tracks, trailing from the place he stood, down the slope, along the valley bottom, between the trees and on and on. Two sets of feet, a wolverine and a child, walking together into the lovely wild.

LIMERICK CITY AND COUNTY

LIBRARY

Nicola Davies

Nicola is an award-winning author, whose many books for children include *The Promise* (Green Earth Book Award 2015, CILIP Kate Greenaway Medal Shortlist 2015), *Tiny* (AAAS/Subaru SB&F Prize 2015), *A First Book of Nature, Whale Boy* (Blue Peter Book Awards Shortlist 2014), and the Heroes of the Wild series (Portsmouth Book Award 2014).

She graduated in Zoology, studied whales and bats and then worked for the BBC Natural History Unit. Underlying all Nicola's writing is the belief that a relationship with nature is essential to every human being, and that now, more than ever, we need to renew that relationship.

Nicola's children's books from Graffeg include *Perfect*, the Shadows and Light series, *The Word Bird, Animal Surprises* and *Into the Blue.*

Fran Shum

Fran Shum was born in Weston-Super-Mare. She grew up with a bombardment of artistic influences, with both her parents being artists, and on a steady diet of graphic novels and Godzilla movies.

She uses both traditional and digital mediums to communicate a variety of narratives and emotions within her work, specialising in artwork for bands and tattoo designs as a freelance illustrator.

The cult movie posters she has designed have become very popular and she has exhibited these in a variety of venues across the UK. Lately she has also taken the time to create work for younger audiences; she has thoroughly enjoyed the change of pass that the recent collaboration with Nicola Davies has produced.

Books in the series

The White Hare
Nicola Davies
Illustrated by Anastasia Izlesou

Mother Cary's Butter Knife
Nicola Davies
Illustrations by Anja Uhren

Elias Martin
Nicola Davies
Illustrations by Fran Shum

The Selkie's Mate
Nicola Davies
Illustrations by Claire Jenkins

Bee Boy and the Moonflowers
Nicola Davies

The Eel Question
Nicola Davies